BLACKBERRY FARM

MOTHER HEN AND MARY

Jane Pilgrim

This edition first published in the United Kingdom in 1999 by
Brockhampton Press
20 Bloomsbury Street
London WC1B 3QA
a member of the Hodder Headline PLC Group

Designed and Produced for Brockhampton Press by
Open Door Limited
80 High Street, Colsterworth, Lincolnshire, NG33 5JA

Illustrator: F. Stocks May
Colour separation: GA Graphics Stamford

Title: BLACKBERRY FARM, Mother Hen and Mary
ISBN: 1-84186-012-3

MOTHER HEN AND MARY

Jane Pilgrim

Illustrated by F. Stocks May

BROCKHAMPTON PRESS

Mother Hen was a kind, brown bird who lived with her baby chick, Mary, at Blackberry Farm. She was rather a fussy hen, but she was kind, and everybody liked her.

But Mary was not always a good chick, and poor Mother Hen used to get very upset when Mary was lost, or when she did something dreadful like hopping into the middle of Mrs Smiles's dough on baking day. Mrs Smiles was the farmer's wife, and she always baked in the big kitchen at Blackberry Farm every Friday morning.

Mrs Smiles was very nice about
that, and told Mother Hen not to
be upset. "I'm sure Mary won't do
it again," she said, "and I will try
to remember to shut the kitchen
door next time." And she gave
Mother Hen a nice piece of crusty
bread to cheer her up.

Another day Mother Hen could not find Mary anywhere when it was bedtime, and it was Rusty the Sheep-dog who told her that he had seen Mary down in the field playing with Mrs Nibble's baby bunnies.

Then Mother Hen was very cross indeed. "You are a very naughty little chick," she scolded, after she had fetched Mary back. "You must stay with me until you are big enough to look after yourself." And she gave Mary a sharp peck with her beak.

Of course Mary cried then. "I
will be a good chick. I will, I will, I
will!" she promised her mother.
But the next day she ran off on
her own again, this time she went
to see what Walter Duck was doing
down by the pond.

Walter was paddling in the pond, looking for something exciting to eat. "Go away, Mary," he quacked. "You'll upset my dinner." But Mary took no notice, and cheaped excitedly at him from the bank. This new world was very strange and very exciting.

Poor Mother Hen found her
there at tea-time. "You naughty,
naughty chick," she scolded, "I
shall have to keep you shut up in
the stable until you are good."

The next day Mother Hen left Mary shut in the stable and went to find Emily the Goat. Emily was wise. Emily would tell her what to do. "It is very difficult, Emily," she clucked; "Mrs Smiles will expect me to start laying eggs again soon, and how can I settle to do that when Mary is so naughty?"

Emily was very helpful. "I think you should go and see Ernest Owl," she said. "He is thinking of starting a school, and if he would take Mary every morning, you would be able to lay your eggs then." "Thank you very much, Emily," said Mother Hen. "I think that is a very good idea. I will go and talk to Ernest Owl."

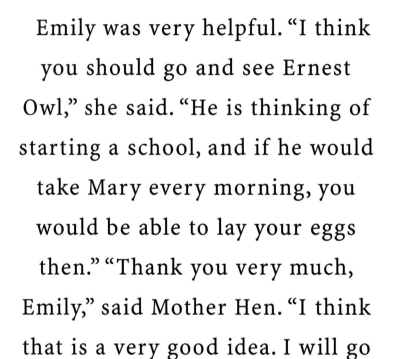

That evening, when Mary had gone to sleep, Mother Hen slipped out of the stable and across the yard to the big oak tree at the edge of the field where Ernest Owl lived. He was sitting on a low branch watching the moon come up behind the farm.

"I hear you are going to start a school, Ernest Owl," she called. 'If you do, can I send my Mary to you in the mornings, because I must have some time to lay my eggs, and she is a naughty little chick and won't stay quietly at home with me?"

Ernest Owl looked very solemn and very wise sitting on his branch in the moonlight. "Yes Mother Hen," he hooted slowly. "You may send your Mary to me when I start my school. I will let you know which day. I think it is time we had a school at Blackberry Farm for all these young things." The next morning Mother Hen told Mary that she was going to send her to school, and Mary was so excited that she hopped up and down and talked about it all day.

"I'm going to school, I'm going to school!" she cheeped to Joe Robin when he looked in at dinner-time; "and I shall learn to grow into a big hen like Mummy and lay lots of eggs." And Mother Hen felt very happy, and began to fuss cheerfully round the stable looking for a nice place where she could lay all the eggs she wanted for the kind people who lived at Blackberry Farm.